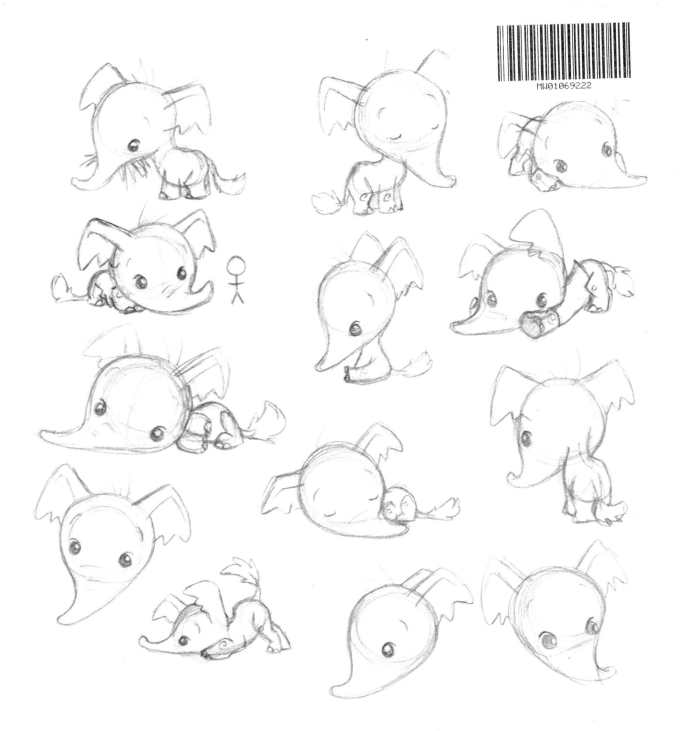

Library of Congress-in-Publication Data
Crofts, III, James D.
The Eloraphant / By James D. Crofts II ; illustrated by Courtney Cope
Summary: A Father discovers his daughter has turned into an elephant.
ISBN-13: 978-1517369835
ISBN-10: 1517369835

To Elora, Wiliam, and Ethan.
My beloved children.
James Crofts

For Mom and Dad, for letting
me be an animal.
Court Cope

The Eloraphant

written by James Crofts
Illustrated by Courtney Cope

Daddy was working on some papers one day when...

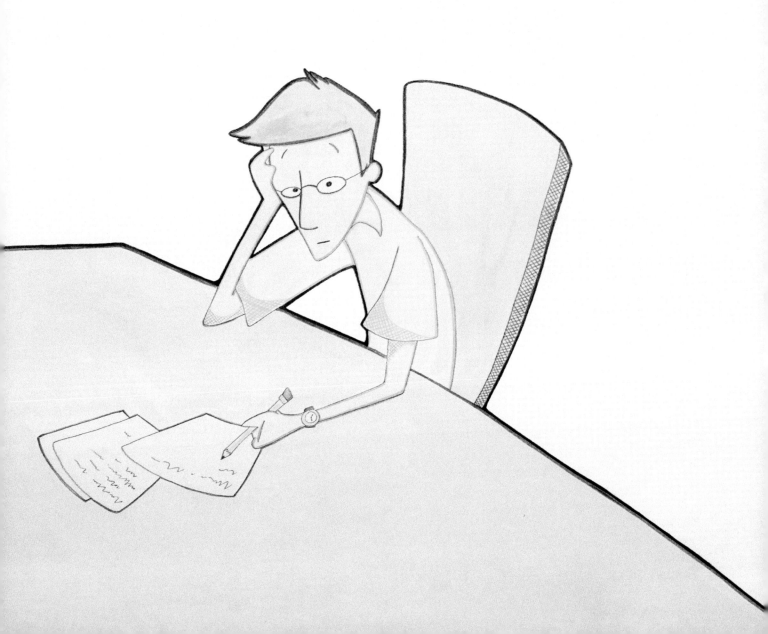

BOOM! THUD!
CRASH! WHAM!
KAPING!

He hurried to Elora's room and found...

...she had turned into an elephant!

She had a furry purple tail...

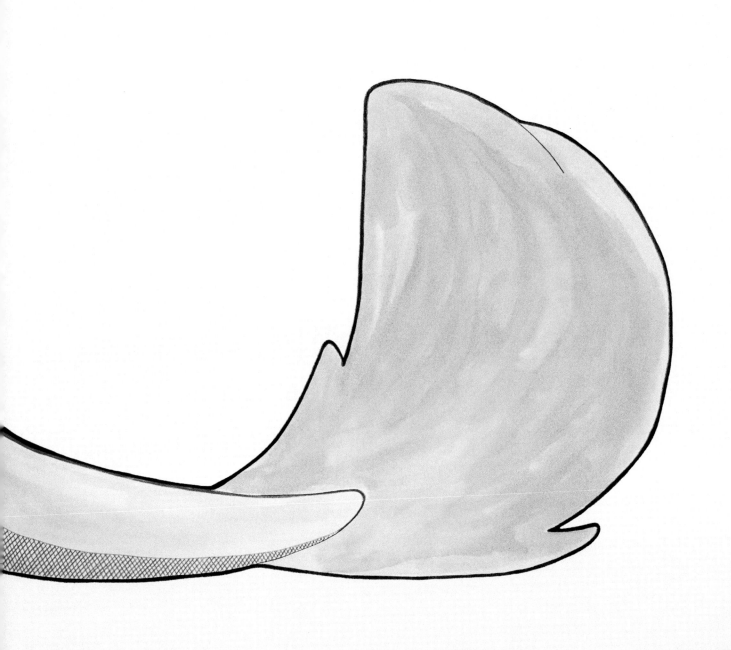

She had a trunk...

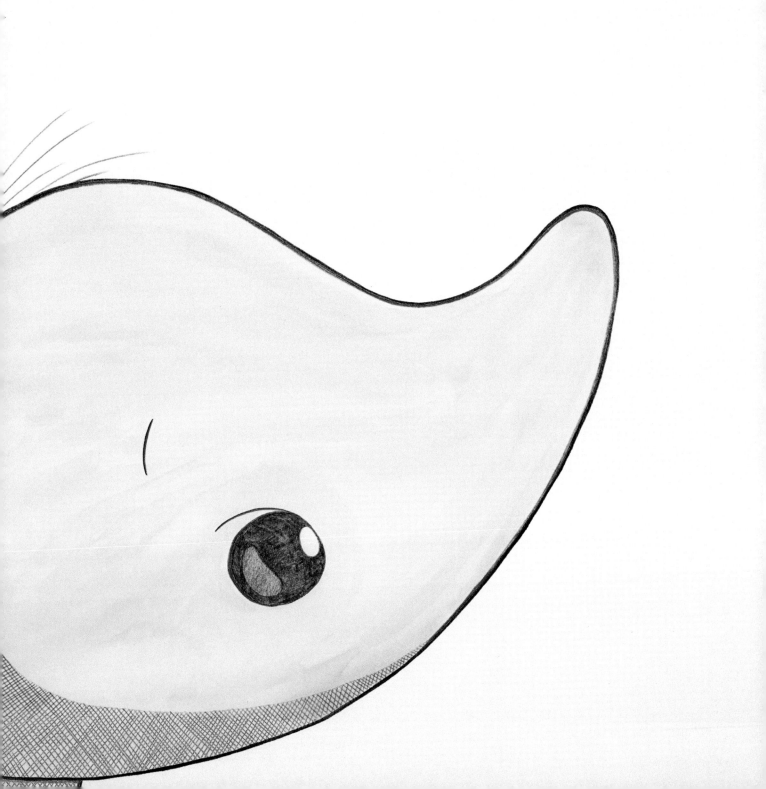

And big perky ears.

"Elora! What happened to you?"
Daddy asked.

"Oh, hello, Daddy," Elora said.

Elora was having a tea party. "Oh, my...uh, you're really...big, aren't you?" Daddy began.

"Would you like some tea?"
she asked.
"But...this is water?" Daddy
replied.

"I know, but I don't tell my dolls. They think it's a tea party," Eloraphant whispered to him.

Then he looked at his watch. "Well, we'd better get you ready for school."

"Can you clean up your toys, please?" Daddy asked. Eloraphant sprang into action. "Sure thing, Daddy!"

After her toys were cleaned up, Daddy helped her get dressed.

Then he brushed her hair.

Daddy gave her breakfast.

He then helped her brush her teeth.

Daddy then tried to get her into the truck.

Daddy tried to push her in.
But he had a better plan.

That is how she rode to school.

When they arrived, all the kids were playing.

Daddy gave Eloraphant her lunch box.

"I love you, Eloraphant."

Eloraphant then went off to school.

James Crofts grew up on a small orchard where he had many grand adventures with his dog. He built many tree houses, club houses, and underground forts. Some of which still exist...

Court Cope was a different animal every day as a child, and then channeled that into drawings. A fan of the quirky and sometimes macabre, Court collects animal skulls, loves dinosaurs and monsters, and is an aspiring parkourist.

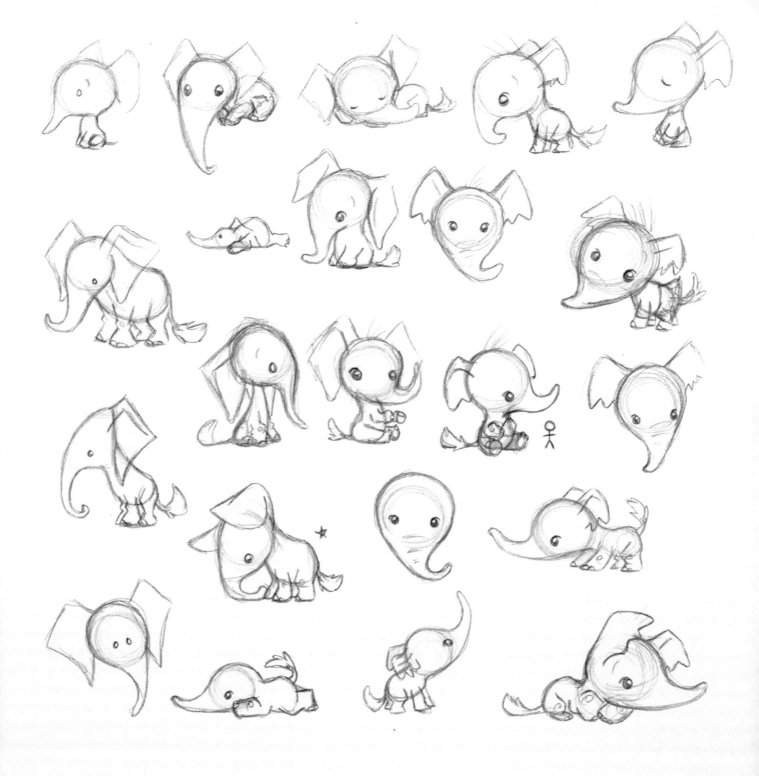

Made in the USA
Las Vegas, NV
30 August 2021